Rudolph Giuliani

By Wil Mara

Consultant
Jeanne Clidas, Ph.D.
National Reading Consultant
and
Professor of Reading, SUNY Brockport

Children's Press®
A Division of Scholastic Inc.
New York Toronto London Auckland Sydney
Mexico City New Delhi Hong Kong
Danbury, Connecticut

Designer: Herman Adler Design
Photo Researcher: Caroline Anderson
The photo on the cover shows Rudolph Giuliani.

Library of Congress Cataloging-in-Publication Data

Mara, Wil.
  Rudolph Giuliani / by Wil Mara.
    p. cm. — (Rookie biographies)
  Includes index.
  Summary: Presents a brief look at the life of one of New York City's
  most popular mayors.
    ISBN 0-516-22860-9 (lib. bdg.)   0-516-27841-X (pbk.)
    1. Giuliani, Rudolph W.—Juvenile literature. 2. Mayors—New York
  (State)—New York—Biography—Juvenile literature. [1. Giuliani, Rudolph
  W. 2. Mayors.] I. Title. II. Series: Rookie biography.
  F128.57.G58 M37 2003
  974.7'1043'092—dc21

                              2002015140

CHILDREN'S PRESS, AND ROOKIE BIOGRAPHIES™, and associated
logos are trademarks and or registered trademarks of Grolier Publishing
Co., Inc. SCHOLASTIC and associated logos are trademarks and or
registered trademarks of Scholastic Inc.
1 2 3 4 5 6 7 8 9 10 R 12 11 10 09 08 07 06 05 04 03

No one loves New York City
more than Rudy Giuliani.

He was born in Brooklyn,
New York, on May 28, 1944.

When he was young, he showed great interest in law. Laws are rules we all have to follow.

8

Giuliani went to New York University School of Law in 1965. He was a good student.

After school, Giuliani worked
as a lawyer for many years.
First, he worked in New York.

Then he moved to Washington, D.C., to work for Ronald Reagan in 1981. Reagan was the President of the United States.

Giuliani came back to New York in 1983. It was where he really wanted to be.

13

Giuliani saw that crime was getting worse in New York. When someone breaks a law, it is called a crime.

Giuliani wanted to stop crime. He wanted New York to be a safe place for everyone to live.

15

16

In 1989, Giuliani decided to get involved in politics. A politician (pol-uh-TISH-uhn) is someone who helps to run a town, state, or country.

Giuliani wanted to be the mayor of New York City.

The mayor is in charge of how the city is run. New York City is very big. The mayor does a lot of work.

Mary Endres Elementary School
Woodstock, IL   19

20

Giuliani did not get to be mayor on his first try. He lost the race for mayor to a man named David Dinkins.

So, Giuliani tried again in 1993.

He won the race the second time.

Giuliani worked hard to stop crime in New York City. He hired more police. He made tougher laws.

The city became a better place. Giuliani was happy about this. He was helping to improve the city he cared about.

When New York City was attacked on September 11, 2001, many people died. Giuliani worked hard to bring everyone together.

Giuliani is no longer the
mayor of New York City.
He is remembered as one of
the greatest mayors the city
ever had.

He did such a good job that
some people call him "The
Mayor of America."

29

Words You Know

Rudy Giuliani

David Dinkins

lawyer

mayor

30

New York City

politician

Ronald Reagan

police

31

Index

About the Author

More than fifty published books bear Wil Mara's name. He has written both fiction and nonfiction, for both children and adults. He lives with his family in northern New Jersey.

Photo Credits